PHINEAS L. MACGUIRE . . .

BLASTS OFF!

by FRANCES O'ROARK DOWELL

illustrated by PRESTON McDANIELS

Atheneum Books for Young Readers

New York   London   Toronto   Sydney

• ATHENEUM BOOKS FOR YOUNG READERS • An imprint of Simon & Schuster Children's Publishing Division • 1230 Avenue of the Americas, New York, New York 10020 •
This book is a work of fiction. Any references to historical events, real people, or real locales are used fictitiously. Other names, characters, places, and incidents are products of the author's imagination, and any resemblance to actual events or locales or persons, living or dead, is entirely coincidental.
• ATHENEUM BOOKS FOR YOUNG READERS is a registered trademark of Simon & Schuster, Inc. • For information about special discounts for bulk purchases, please contact Simon & Schuster Special Sales at 1-866-506-1949 or business@simonandschuster.com. • The Simon & Schuster Speakers Bureau can bring authors to your live event. For more information or to book an event, contact the Simon & Schuster Speakers Bureau at 1-866-248-3049 or visit our website at www.simonspeakers.com. • Also available in an Atheneum Books for Young Readers hardcover edition • Book design by Sonia Chaghatzbanian and Michael McCartney • The text for this book is set in GarthGraphic. • The illustrations for this book were rendered in pencil. • Manufactured in the United States of America • 0511 OFF • First Atheneum Books for Young Readers paperback edition June 2011 • 10 9 8 7 6 5 4 3 2 1 • The Library of Congress has cataloged the hardcover edition as follows: • Dowell, Frances O'Roark. • Phineas L. MacGuire . . . blasts off! / Frances O'Roark Dowell; illustrated by Preston McDaniels. —1st ed. • p. cm. • Summary: Hoping to earn money to attend Space Camp, fourth-grade science whiz Phineas MacGuire gets a job as a dog walker, then enlists the aid of his friends Ben and Aretha to help with experiments using the dog's "slobber." • ISBN 978-1-4169-2689-4 (hc) • [1. Moneymaking projects—Fiction. 2. Science—Experiments—Fiction. 3. Dogs—Fiction. 4. Schools—Fiction. 5. Friendship—Fiction.] I. McDaniels, Preston, ill. II. Title PZ7.D75455Phb 2008 • [Fic]—dc22 • 2007030162 • ISBN 978-1-4424-2204-9 (pbk) • ISBN 978-1-4424-2394-7 (eBook)

Other books by Frances O'Roark Dowell

Phineas L. MacGuire . . . Erupts!

Phineas L. MacGuire . . . Gets Slimed!

Dovey Coe

Where I'd Like to Be

The Secret Language of Girls

Chicken Boy

Shooting the Moon

The Kind of Friends We Used to Be

Falling In

Ten Miles Past Normal

To Spencer Graham, Sam Loyack,
and Aidan Paul—great friends,
smart guys

—F. O. D.

The author would like to thank
the following people for their support,
wisdom and *joie de vivre*: Caitlyn Dlouhy;
Kiley Fitzsimmons; Amy Graham; Danielle Paul;
Tom, Kathryn, and Megan Harris; and Clifton,
Jack, and Will Dowell. She would like to thank
T. J. Mukundan for his insights about Space Camp.

PHINEAS L. MACGUIRE . . .

BLASTS OFF!

⚗ chapter one

My name is Phineas Listerman MacGuire.

Feel free to call me Mac.

Some people even call me Big Mac, since I'm tall for my age.

I don't mind being called Phin or Phineas. I had a soccer coach last year who only called me MacGuire.

I thought that was sort of cool.

He never called me Listerman, in

case you were wondering.

No one calls me Listerman. Not unless they want to get seriously slimed.

I am a scientist. In fact, I am probably the best fourth-grade scientist in all of Woodbrook Elementary School. I am an expert in the following areas of scientific inquiry:

1. All molds and fungi, particularly slime molds of every variety
2. Volcanoes and other things that explode
3. Bug identification

Up until yesterday I had no idea that I was a potential scientific genius when it came to astronomy, which is, if you didn't know, the study of planets and stars and everything up in space.

Don't get me wrong. I have read at least sixty-seven astronomy books and am famous for having eaten a board book about the planets when I was two.

It's just astronomy wasn't one of my big things.

Until I heard about Space Camp.

It all started with Stacey Windham, and Share and Stare.

You would think that as a scientist, I would know five hundred times as much about space as Stacey Windham, a bossy girl in my class who thinks she is the queen and has never once shown any interest in anything besides being mean to people.

So how did she know that there are earthquakes on Mars before I did?

Except on Mars they're called Marsquakes.

You'd think I would have heard about that.

"Some scientists think that Mars at one time had titanic plates in it, just like Earth does," Stacey reported for Share and Stare yesterday morning. Share and Stare is what Mrs. Tuttle, our teacher, has instead of Show and Tell. For Share and Stare you have to bring something that's connected to what we're studying at school. We have just started a unit on space, and Stacey waved an article torn out of a magazine while she talked.

"I'm interested in titanic plates because I have seen the movie *Titanic* four times," Stacey continued. "Even though it is rated PG-13."

A bunch of girls gasped. I raised my hand. Stacey nodded at me like she was the teacher.

"I think you mean 'tectonic plates,'" I informed her. "Tectonic plates are what shift around and cause earthquakes."

"Well, I've still seen *Titanic* four times. And it's rated PG-13." Stacey sneered at me. "I bet you've never seen one single PG-13 movie."

Half of my classmates waved their hands in the air. "Oooh! I have! I have!"

Later I asked Stacey where she'd found the article, and she showed me a copy of a magazine called *Astronomy*. "It's my dad's," she said. "He has a telescope. Except he's always too busy to use it. Sometimes when I have a slumber party, we use it for spying on the people who live across the street."

I sighed. Leave it to Stacey Windham to take a perfectly good scientific tool like a telescope and use it for evil.

Tonight at dinner I asked my mom if we could get a subscription to *Astronomy* magazine. She gave me her best I Spend Ten Zillion Dollars a Year on Stuff for You Already look and shook her head. "You get plenty of magazines." She listed them on her fingers: *"National Geographic Kids, Scientific American, Ranger Rick . . ."*

"To be honest, I think I'm getting kind of old for Ranger Rick. Maybe we could trade that subscription for one to *Astronomy.*"

"Too old for *Ranger Rick?*" My mom looked stunned. "I read *Ranger Rick* until I was twelve years old. You're never too old for *Ranger Rick!*"

My stepdad, Lyle, grabbed another piece of pizza from the box on the middle of the table. "You know, I saw something in the paper the other day about a Space

Camp they have down in Alabama. I think it's connected to NASA. The kids do a lot of stuff on Mars exploration."

I nearly jumped out of my chair. It was like every cell in my body got electrified at the same time. All of the sudden I knew that my life should revolve around the study of astronomy, space, and all things beyond Earth's atmosphere. "Space Camp? Mars exploration? I need to go there immediately!"

"It's pretty expensive," Lyle told me through a mouth full of pizza. "And pretty far away."

"I could save up for it! I've already got twenty-nine dollars saved up for a chemistry set. I could use it for Space Camp instead."

My mom looked doubtful. "I don't know, honey. I think you're a little young for a sleepaway camp. Maybe when you're eleven. Besides, I don't think we can afford to send you to camp this year. The minivan's almost too pooped to pop. It's about time to buy a new one."

Leave it to my mom to put minivans before scientific knowledge.

"What if I pay for everything myself?"

My mom still looked doubtful. "If you saved up enough money for Space Camp—*and* a round-trip plane ticket—

then maybe I'd consider it. Maybe."

I ran around to the other side of the table and hugged my mom. Well, it wasn't really a hug. It was more bumping my shoulder against her shoulder.

We scientists are not big huggers as a rule.

But my mom smiled anyway.

She knows a scientific hug when she gets one.

chapter two

It turns out that a week at Space Camp costs $799.

Or in other words, three and a half years' worth of allowances.

And that's not counting a round-trip plane ticket.

Houston, we have a problem.

"What you need, Mac, is a job," Aretha Timmons told me at recess. I am normally allergic to girls, but for some reason

my immune system can tolerate Aretha Timmons. I think this is because she is a fellow scientist. Plus, she never wears purple.

Purple makes me break out in hives.

So do girls, for that matter.

I don't even want to think about what a purple girl would do to my immune system.

Aretha, being a fellow scientist, was the first person I discussed my Space Camp problem with. She is probably the smartest person in Mrs. Tuttle's fourth-grade class besides me, and rumor has it she has saved every allowance and birthday-card dollar she has ever received in her entire life.

Aretha leaned back on the swing she was sitting on. "I mean, if you want to go to camp over spring break, you've got five months until registration is due, right? Seven hundred and ninety-nine dollars sounds like a lot, but divide it up into small increments, like fifty dollars a week, and suddenly it's a do-able sum."

"How does a nine-year-old make fifty dollars a week?" I shook my head sadly. "It's just not going to happen."

"First thing," Aretha said, holding up a finger, "make a list of your marketable skills. Number two, devise a list of jobs that require your marketable skills. Match the two, and you're on your way to fifty dollars a week."

"You could also sell all your stuff. I bet you'd get five thousand bucks for all your stuff, like your bed and everything."

This came from Ben, who was kneeling in the dirt beside the swing set and making a sculpture out of gravel and sticks.

It appeared to be a *Star Wars* X-wing starfighter, but it might also have been a lopsided birthday cake with a cat taking a nap on top of it.

Sometimes with Ben you have to ask.

Aretha rolled her eyes. "Who's going to pay five thousand dollars for Mac's bed? Is it a golden bed? A bed encrusted with diamonds and rubies?"

"Not just his bed," Ben replied. "His clothes and toys and everything. Plus, his slime mold collection. His slime mold collection alone might get him five hundred. I mean, it's awesome."

I tried to look modest about my slime mold, but Ben was right. If you are looking for the slime mold genius of the universe, well, I'm pretty much it. I had three shelves of mold growing in my bedroom. I'd never thought about their monetary value before, but maybe Ben was on to something.

That slime mold could be worth big bucks.

The problem was, I couldn't sell it in a million years.

The psychological devastation would be too much.

I am very attached to my slime mold.

"First, let me point out that most of Mac's stuff isn't actually Mac's stuff," Aretha said. "The slime mold, yes. The bed? The dresser? The desk? No way. That is the official property of Mac's parents. Put 'em on sale, go to jail."

I don't think my parents would really send me to jail for selling my furniture.

But they might put me in the longest time-out in history.

Ben started constructing a battle droid out of acorns. "Well, if selling his furniture is out of the question, maybe there's something else he can sell." Ben looked up at me. "You could have a lemonade stand."

"I'd have to sell a lot of lemonade to make seven hundred ninety-nine dollars," I told him.

Aretha checked her watch. Her watch isn't just a watch, it is a weather station. It has a hygrometer, which lets you know how much moisture is in the air, a thermometer, and a barometric pressure tendency arrow.

It also tells the time, but who cares?

"I would love to sit here and come up with ideas for Mac," she told us, "but in three minutes and forty-eight seconds I have a meeting with Principal Patino about the Read to Win pizza party."

Aretha is our class president and is often called to the principal's office for important meetings about pizza and whether or not the Girl Scouts should be able to sell cookies in the cafeteria during recess.

Ben, believe it or not, is our class vice president, but he is hardly ever called to the principal's office for important meetings.

He gets called there for other stuff, however.

Aretha stood up and turned to me.

"Like you, Mac, I am a scientific thinker, but I am also an advocate of positive thinking. If you tell yourself that there is a solution to your problem, you will find the solution. If you need a way to make money, tell yourself that you will find a way. Say this every morning when you wake up, and every night before you go to bed. The power of positive thinking is very strong." She held up her wrist. "That's how I got this watch."

"What? You just thought positively about it and—*poof!*—one day the watch appeared?" Ben asked her.

Aretha looked down her nose at Ben and squinted.

She does not appreciate sarcasm.

"No, Mr. Ben Robbins, that is not how it happened. What happened was I saw this watch, I wanted this watch, and I told myself I would get this watch. I thought about it positively for two weeks, and then, with no prompting from me whatsoever, my father offered me a reward if I got straight As two marking periods in a row. That's when I knew I had this watch in the bag, thanks to the power of positive thinking."

"I'll try it," I told Aretha, feeling doubtful. "Anything's worth a try."

All afternoon I tried to think positively. *I will find a way to make money,* I repeated about two thousand times in my head. *I will find a way to make money for Space Camp.* But the whole time I was being Mr. Positive, I felt sort of weird. I respect Aretha as a scientist, but this was not the most scientific method I had ever heard of.

But here's the funny thing: It worked.

🔬 chapter three

Here are just a few reasons I think Mars is a scientifically fascinating place:

1. Mars has the biggest volcano in the whole solar system. It's called Olympus Mons. It's bigger than Mount Everest. It sort of makes me jealous that Mars has such a big volcano, if you want to know the truth, especially since Earth

is a much bigger planet. It's not really fair that Earth's volcanoes are so puny compared to Olympus Mons.

2. Mars has two moons, Deimos and Phobos. They look like potatoes that have been sitting in the kitchen cabinet for too long. One of my goals is to be the first astronaut to walk on Deimos and Phobos. Deimos is only nine miles long. I could probably walk across it in a few hours, which would make my mom happy. She is always telling me to get more exercise.

3. It takes six months to get to Mars from Earth, even though Mars is the next planet over from Earth. If you look at a poster of the solar

system, you'd think it would take maybe a few days to get to Mars, depending on how fast your spaceship was going. Traveling through space for six months would be like a dream come true for me.

4. One Mars year equals 687 Earth days. That means it takes 687 days for Mars to orbit the sun. So a year on Mars would pretty much be like two years on Earth. I figure there must be some way to use all that extra time to my advantage. I could finally reread the entire Mysteries of Planet Zindar series, from book one to book forty-three, for example, or memorize the periodic table of chemical elements, which I have been meaning to do for some time now.

I was thinking about these interesting facts on the bus home from school in between my positive-thinking thoughts about making money to go to Space Camp. I was also thinking how awesome it would be to go to Space Camp and hang out with other kids who liked to contemplate interesting Mars facts. Aretha Timmons is not uninterested in the solar system, but she is more fascinated by things like bacteria and horrible diseases. If you don't catch her in the right mood, she will give a planet like Mars about four seconds of her attention before she changes the subject.

I have tried to get Ben, who is my best friend and smarter than anybody realizes, including Ben, more interested in science, but he is pretty happy just to be a genius artist. Sometimes he will do scientific research when he needs to know something for a comic book he's drawing, and he does have a healthy interest in slime mold.

I could not be best friends with somebody who didn't have a healthy interest in slime mold.

Between the positive-thinking thoughts and the Mars thoughts, I wasn't paying very much attention when the bus pulled up to my stop. I got off the bus and took two steps toward my house.

At which time I was pulverized by a force larger than life.

This force is otherwise known as Lemon Drop, the world's biggest Labrador retriever, who belongs to my approximately eight-thousand-year-old neighbor, Mrs. McClosky. Lemon Drop knocked me down, slobbered all over my best

Museum of Life and Science T-shirt, the green one with the picture of the lunar module on it, and practically strangled me with his leash as he planted wet goopy dog kisses all over my face.

Mrs. McClosky stood on her front steps, holding on desperately to the railing, and called out in her eight-thousand-year-old voice, "Down, Lemon Drop! Leave Cornelius alone!"

Lemon Drop didn't even give her a second look.

He was too busy drowning me with slobber.

I could feel my eyes start to bulge out of my head, which is actually sort of an interesting feeling, except for the part that involves being choked to death. Just as little white dots started floating in front of my eyes, Mrs. McClosky whipped a tennis ball at Lemon Drop, who immediately started looking around to see who was up for a game of catch.

For an approximately eight-thousand-year-old woman, Mrs. McClosky has a pretty good arm.

I slowly stood up, rubbing my neck.

"Oh, dear, I'm so sorry, Atticus," Mrs. McClosky called from her steps. "I was just about to take Lemon Drop for a walk, and he got away from me. Normally I pay a dog walker, but the young man who was helping me quit unexpectedly yesterday. That Tilda Fergus offered him seven dollars an hour to walk her Scottish terrier, Perky. Really, Ulysses, life is so unfair sometimes."

Before I could say anything, Lemon Drop dropped a slobber-soaked tennis ball at my feet.

"You want me to touch that?" I asked him.

Lemon Drop nodded.

"Did you just nod?"

Lemon Drop nodded again.

"He's a very intelligent dog," Mrs. McClosky called. "They say Labradors aren't smart, but they just haven't met my Lemon Drop."

In my many scientific pursuits I have never developed much of an interest in animal psychology. Maybe that's because my mom is allergic to dogs, and I'm allergic to cats, and amphibians of all sorts give Lyle the creeps.

Which is to say, I have not had much hands-on experience with our four-legged and finned and webbed-toed friends.

But you have to admit, a dog who can nod is a pretty interesting scientific specimen.

Mrs. McClosky began tottering toward me. "You wouldn't happen to want an after-school job, would you, Barnabus? I need someone to walk Lemon Drop every afternoon for an hour. I can pay you six dollars."

"A week?"

"A day," Mrs. McClosky said. "My grandson comes over on the weekends to help out, so I would only need you to walk Lemon Drop Monday through Friday."

So, $6 a day, five days a week. That was $30 a week, or $120 a month.

Not enough for Space Camp, but definitely a start.

"I'd be happy to do it," I said, leaning

over and picking up the slobbered-on tennis ball.

A slobbered-on tennis ball is one of the grosser things you can pick up with your bare hands, in case you were wondering.

But for six dollars an hour I'd learn to live with it.

chapter four

"You're getting a dog? Awesome!"

Ben was lying on my bedroom floor eating two-year-old graham sticks from an open pack he'd found under my dresser.

You will always find something to eat in my room. Pretzels, chips, gummy worms, crackers—you name it, I've got it somewhere, usually under my bed or in my top desk drawer.

Freshness is not guaranteed.

"I'm not getting a dog," I said. "I have a job walking a dog. To be precise, I have a job walking Lemon Drop, the biggest Labrador retriever known to humankind."

"My dad had a Saint Bernard growing up," Ben told me, popping one last graham stick in his mouth before sitting up.

"He said it was as big as a truck. And when he shook his head—you know, like if a fly was bugging him?—slobber would fly out five feet in every direction."

"Why do dogs slobber so much?" I asked, scientifically curious. "I mean, what's up with their saliva glands?"

Ben thought about this for a second. "But have you ever noticed little dogs don't really slobber very much? It's like they're too hyper to slobber."

I have noticed since Ben and I have been best friends that he doesn't make many scientific observations, but when he does, they are always interesting and worth investigating.

"Let's get Sarah to Google it," I said, jumping up from my bed. "There's got to be an answer to dog slobber."

Sarah P. Fortemeyer is my babysitter.

More specifically, she is the Babysitter from Outer Space, only not the good kind.

However, she is the only person in the house from 3:00 to 5:30 p.m. who has access to my mom's computer and permission to go online.

"You want me to Google 'slobber'?" Sarah was sitting at the kitchen table, reading a Teenage Girl Space Alien magazine and talking on her cell phone at the same time. "They want me to Google 'slobber,'" she said into the phone. After a pause she said, "Yeah, I know, but I need the money and his little sister is really nice."

She made a few more remarks into the phone that I was pretty sure weren't compliments about me and Ben, and then headed for my mom's computer, which was on the counter next to the fridge.

"You probably need to be more scientifically specific than just 'slobber,'" I told her. "You probably need to put something like 'dog saliva.'"

Sarah logged on to the Internet, brought up the Google page, typed in the phrase "dog saliva," then hit enter. "Hey, here's something about dog saliva being a wonder drug," she said after a second, finally sounding interested. "Some kids are doing a science fair project about it. They think it might kill bacteria."

I felt automatically jealous that some-one who wasn't me had come up with such a scientifically amazing science fair topic.

"Oooh, and here's something about how dog saliva might be cleaner than human saliva."

"I've heard that before!" Ben exclaimed. "It's better to be kissed by a dog than by a human because you'll get more germs from the human."

"But what about the amount of saliva produced?" I asked.

"Hmmm," Sarah said, scrolling down the page. "Oh, hey, here's something. It says that dogs that eat dry food pro-duce more-watery saliva than dogs that eat meat. Meat-eating dogs have more-mucusy saliva."

You could tell by the expression on

her face that all of the sudden Sarah Fortemeyer wasn't that interested in dog saliva anymore.

Ben, on the other hand, was fascinated.

"Yeah, that makes perfect sense! Because think about it, it's sort of like humans, like when we eat crackers? Or when we eat a hamburger. You definitely have different spit after a hamburger than after a cracker."

He turned to me. "You've got to admit it, Mac, that would make an interesting science fair topic for next year."

Ben and I made a volcano for the fourth-grade science fair. We got an honorable mention. It was one of the greatest scientific disappointments of my life, although my mom keeps telling me the important thing is that Ben and I did our best.

It is that sort of attitude that could cause a person to go his whole life and never win a Nobel Prize in Physics.

Sarah continued to scroll, but she was shaking her head. "I'm not finding anything about quantities of dog saliva," she said. "Mostly what's here is about bacteria in dog saliva or else how some people are allergic to dog saliva."

I was disappointed but not defeated.

I had not yet begun to research dog slobber.

And now with Lemon Drop, I had a subject right around the corner.

That's when it hit me: not only did I have a job, I also had a walking, nodding, slobbering science lab at my disposal.

Science lab.

Science Lab.

Lemon Drop the Science Lab.

As in *Lab*rador retriever?

I started laughing so hard that Sarah P. Fortemeyer had to get me a glass of water and Ben smacked me on the back about a hundred times.

Boy, sometimes I crack myself up.

🔅 chapter five

Aretha was less interested in dog slobber and more interested in the fact that Lemon Drop could nod his head yes.

"That is a very unusual trait in a *Canis familiaris*," she told me from across the cafeteria aisle during lunch period on Monday. In the fourth grade it is against the law for boys and girls to sit together in the cafeteria. You can talk on the playground, but there is something about eating together that rubs people the wrong way. The punishment for breaking the law is a lifetime of other kids saying, "Oh, Mac and Aretha are going to get married," or, "Where's your girlfriend Aretha, Mac?" So I sit at a boys' table, and Aretha sits at the girls' table next to it, and we have conversations without actually looking at each other.

"Yeah, I know," I told her, pulling off the crust of my tuna fish sandwich. "I did a bunch of research this weekend, and even though there's lots of documentation about how dogs are really smart, I couldn't find anything about dogs nodding their head for yes."

Aretha blew some air through her straw. "Add that to the fact that Labrador retrievers aren't supposed to be very bright."

"That's misinformation," I informed

her. "I found this list of the smartest dogs, and Labs were, like, number eight out of, like, eighty breeds. They are completely underestimated, intelligence-wise."

"I stand corrected," Aretha said. "My apologies to Labrador retrievers everywhere."

"The problem is, I don't even know how to start running experiments about Lemon Drop's intelligence. I was thinking that it would be better to focus on slobber. I mean, it's just easier to run experiments on, for one thing—"

"And for another thing, we could film it." Ben plopped down next to me, dropping his yellow tray on the table and spilling his milk everywhere. "I just had a fantastizoid idea standing in line. I've got a video camera, right?"

I nodded. Ben's dad gave him a digital

camcorder for becoming our class's vice president. He was hoping Ben would drop his dream of being the world's greatest comic-book artist and become a visual media whiz instead.

"So all the sudden it came to me: Let's document the life of Lemon Drop. Either we end up making some great discovery about dog slobber, or else we can sell our documentary to the Animal Channel or Disney. They love dog stuff. Any way you look at it, we make big bucks. You can go to Space Camp, and I can go to the annual World Comic Book Convention in Honolulu, Hawaii."

Ben got a dreamy look on his face. His dream has always been to go to Hawaii and learn to surf. He feels that surfing should be part of every genius comic-book artist's lifestyle.

From the corner of my eye I could see Aretha get an excited look on her face, which meant her brain was running full steam ahead. "We'll build a multimedia website," she suddenly exclaimed, practically hopping up and down in her seat. "We'll upload digital footage of Lemon Drop, post charts and graphs, even run experiments on his saliva. It will be magnificent."

She actually turned and looked straight at me, risking a lifetime of ridicule from our peers. "I'm going to get a badge out of this. Maybe two, maybe three."

Aretha's goal is to be the most successful Girl Scout that Woodbrook Elementary School has ever produced. She has only been a Girl Scout for two and a half months, but I'm pretty sure she's already halfway there. So far she has gotten badges for making penicillin (with my help), starting a community garden in her neighborhood, rock climbing, auto repair, cooking, and creating her own blog ("Because I Say So, by Aretha Timmons"), which she updates daily. If there is a badge for being elected president of the United States before you turn ten, Aretha will probably get that one too.

I crunched on a baby carrot, wondering if Ben's idea would actually work. I had never heard of fourth-grade filmmakers before. On top of that, it was hard to believe anyone would be that interested in watching a movie about Lemon Drop slobbering.

On the other hand, I'd never figured out why people liked to watch movies about other people kissing each other and holding hands.

I mean, who can explain the public's viewing tastes?

And what if we made a great scientific documentary and got rich from it? What if we came up with some great discovery about dog slobber? I'd be able to go to Space Camp, maybe for the entire summer, not just over spring break. In my backpack I had the Space Camp brochure I'd downloaded from the website. It was all there: spaceship simulators, rocket launches, robotics, life on a space station. By the end of just one week I'd practically be a certified astronaut.

I pounded Ben on the back. "Let's do it!"

Aretha high-fived the air. "Yes!"

Ben grinned. "This is going to be awesome."

◎ chapter six

This afternoon Sarah P. Fortemeyer
drove me and my little sister, Margaret,
to the library, which she always does on
Mondays after I get home from school.
Normally it is one of the highlights of
my week. Mrs. Zelinski, the children's
librarian, always has at least one great
science book recommendation for me.

But today I wanted to get to my dog-
walking job and start making important

scientific discoveries about Lemon Drop. I had already come up with two experiments I wanted to try:

1. Collect at least three samples of saliva. The first sample would be collected midway through our walk, by which time Lemon Drop should have worked up a mouthful of slobber. The second sample would be collected after Lemon Drop and I had played five minutes of slobberball, and the third one would be taken after Lemon Drop drank from his water dish. I would collect each sample in a different vial (or olive jars I'd taken from the recycling bin, whichever was more handy) and then view them

through the microscope my dad had given me for my birthday. I would examine the samples to see which one was the stringiest, which one was the wateriest, and which one was just the plain grossest.

2. Test Lemon Drop's slobber for chemical reactions. What would happen if I mixed slobber with vinegar? With baking soda? Would it fizz? Was it possible to make slobber blow up? Would certain chemicals cause slobber to change colors? Was it possible that my mom would finally let me buy a chemistry set to test slobber's chemical properties if I explained to her the importance of slobber science and how

I would probably make great scientific breakthroughs if I just had the right tools to work with?

Probably not. But it was worth a try.

I think experiments are the coolest part of being a scientist. And for the first time I was realizing that making up your own experiments is extra cool. If you can't find any research on why dogs slobber so much, you do your own research. Nobody can stop you. Nobody can say, "No, you can't do that."

That is a rare event in the life of a nine-year-old boy.

When we walked into the children's section of the library, Mrs. Zelinski noticed me right away. "I have an amazing book for you, Mac," she told me, reaching under her desk and pulling something out. "Just got it today, and as soon as I saw it, I thought, 'This is a book for Mac MacGuire.'"

She handed the book to me. I couldn't believe it: The title was *Mars Comes to Earth: Experiments for Kids*. I immediately took a seat at my favorite table and started reading. I skipped over a bunch of the introductory junk and zoomed through the pages, looking for experiments where stuff exploded.

It turns out that Mars is not a particularly explosive planet.

After reading the book for about ten minutes, I started to see that in some ways Mars was a sort of quiet planet. It's not like you're going to hop over there and find a lot of activities going on. In fact, the big thing in Mars exploration, according to *Mars Comes to Earth*, is seeing if you can find tiny little bits of bacteria that would prove maybe life exists on Mars, or that at least it existed at some point in Martian history.

The good thing about being a scientist is that after you get over the disappointment that nothing is going to explode, you can still get pretty interested in a scientific topic. I mean, all of the sudden I actually started to care about whether or not microscopic bacteria lived on Mars. It became this automatic big thing with me.

I found two experiments I was going to start right away:

1. The "Is There Life on Mars?" experiment. What you do is take three jars and fill each one about halfway with sand. Then you put two teaspoons of baking powder in one jar, two teaspoons of salt in the next jar, and two teaspoons of yeast in the third jar (don't forget to label the jars). You refrigerate the jars overnight so they get cold like Mars, and the next day you add warm sugar water to each jar and see what reaction you get. If you get a slow, steady reaction, then you know there's life in the jar. This is like the experiments the

Viking 2 probe did on Martian soil.

2. The "Why Is Mars Red?" experiment. You need more sand, some steel wool, and a pair of gloves, since steel wool can be sharp. You pour the sand into a pan, cut up the steel wool and mix it with the sand. Then you pour water over the sand and steel wool, enough to cover everything. You leave the pan somewhere where your two-year-old sister won't knock the whole thing over, and every day you check it to see what color it turns to.

I walked up to the desk and handed Mrs. Z. the book and my card. "I'll take it," I told her.

"I thought you would," she replied. While she was checking out the book, she asked, "So, what interesting projects are you up to these days, Mac?"

I think it's possible that Mrs. Z. herself is a scientist disguised as a mild-mannered librarian. I have noticed she takes a special interest in my scientific work.

This is not true of all the adults I have met in my lifetime.

I told her about Space Camp, and I told her about the Lemon Drop experiments. Mrs. Z. nodded as she listened. "You know, I think they used to send dogs into space," she told me. "The Soviets definitely did, way back at the beginning of the space programs."

I tried to imagine living in a space shuttle with Lemon Drop. I imagined big blobs of drool in the antigravity atmosphere, floating around like little lost planets.

"Do they still do that?" I asked, sort of worried. As a future astronaut, I was willing to put up with a lot of discomfort, but I wasn't sure I was willing to put up with floating dog spit.

Mrs. Z. handed me my book. "I don't think so. Now they send monkeys."

I imagined a space shuttle filled with monkeys. I wondered if I was allergic to monkeys. I am allergic to thirteen things, including all nuts, cats, yogurt, and lipstick. If I had to guess, I'd say I'm allergic to floating monkeys, too.

Being an astronaut was going to be a lot more demanding than I'd ever thought.

chapter seven

It didn't take long for the slobber thing to get out of control.

Part one of the slobber adventure was pretty simple. Test Lemon Drop's saliva at different times to see how it changed. All that was going to take was three jars and some Popsicle sticks.

"And crackers," Ben said when we were sitting in his room coming up with our slobber plan. "I had this idea that

Lemon Drop could eat some crackers, and I could eat some crackers, and then we'd collect slobber from both of us and compare it."

"You're going to spit cracker-spit in a jar?" I asked. I don't know why, but the idea of studying Ben's spit kind of grossed me out. Dog slobber was cool. Human slobber? I don't think so.

"Yeah," Ben said. "Compare and contrast, like Mrs. Tuttle is always telling us to do."

The whole time we'd been talking, Ben had been working on his latest comic book, "Derek the Destroyer and the Slime Creatures from Outer Space." I am happy to report that the Slime Creatures are good guys who help Derek the Destroyer out. I leaned over and pointed to one of the slime guys who needed a

little more green. "That's when we're writing stuff for language arts," I said as Ben inked the spot I'd pointed to. "Like compare and contrast soccer and football, or compare and contrast spring and fall."

"Exactly!" Ben exclaimed. He put down

his marker. "And compare and contrast my spit and Lemon Drop's."

I had to think fast. I am a scientist, not a grossologist. "I think it would be more scientific to compare Lemon Drop's slobber with the slobber of other dogs. Different breeds of dogs. The only problem is I don't know any other dogs personally."

Ben grinned. "I've got an idea."

First things first: Lemon Drop. After school the next day Ben and Aretha rode the school bus home with me. Aretha claimed she still was not interested in slobber. However, she felt she might be able to fulfill some requirements of her Pet Care badge by spending time with Lemon Drop.

"We do not have pets in our home," Aretha explained to me and Ben as we got off the bus. "My parents have busy professional lives, and my sister and brother and I have too many important extracurricular activities to responsibly care for a pet."

"So you're going to try to pass off Lemon Drop as your dog so you can get a badge?" Ben teased her.

"No, I am not," said Aretha. If Aretha were the sort of person to punch another person in the arm, I think she would have whacked Ben at that moment. However, Aretha is not a puncher. She is a scientist. "I am going to bond with Lemon Drop, and after we bond, we will participate together in a number of activities that will enable me to honestly report I have a relationship with a canine creature. Just because I don't own Lemon Drop doesn't mean we can't be friends."

Aretha's first activity with Lemon Drop was to get him to drink a bowl of water so we could get a sample of watery slobber for our experiments.

"Okay, nice doggie," she said, grabbing Lemon Drop by his collar and dragging him to his water bowl on Mrs. McClosky's deck. "I hope you're thirsty."

At first Lemon Drop seemed more interested in sniffing Aretha's knees, which were completely new to him, than drinking from his water bowl. Mrs. McClosky, who had been watching from her back door, came out with a box of doggie treats.

"Here, Athena, dear," she said, handing the box to Aretha. "Give him one or two of these. My Lemon Drop is always thirsty after he has some treats."

"Thank you, Mrs. McClosky," Aretha

said, taking a few treats from the box. She turned to Lemon Drop. "Here you go, Lemon Drop, a treat from me to you."

Lemon Drop jumped up and nuzzled Aretha's hands to get the treats, which made Aretha giggle, which is not a typical Aretha thing to do. "I had no idea bonding would be this much fun," she said, sounding surprised.

Just like Mrs. McClosky had predicted, as soon as Lemon Drop had eaten his treats, he lapped up his bowl of water.

Now all I had to do was get him to spit in the jar I was holding.

Ben held his camcorder up to his eye and started to talk in a loud whisper, like he was doing a voice-over for a TV show. "Okay, everybody, here's the world-famous scientist Phineas L. 'Mac' MacGuire, about to get a bunch of slobber from Lemon Drop, the amazing Labrador retriever. Can he do it? Can he make Lemon Drop spit up some good old saliva in the name of scientific research?"

At first I thought the answer to that was a big, fat no. I held out the jar under Lemon Drop's mouth, but Lemon Drop wasn't interested. He was too busy making goo-goo eyes at Aretha, probably hoping she would give him another treat.

And while he was making goo-goo eyes, thick drops of slobber were dribbling off his lips. Every time I tried to catch them, he'd fling his head around, and instead of getting slobber in the jar, I got it all over my shirt.

And ears.

And face.

I didn't know whether to try to catch the slobber in midair or to go home and take a bath.

And then I had a scientific-genius sort of thought.

If I could get Lemon Drop to lick the inside of the jar, some slobber was sure to fall in there.

"Mrs. McClosky, could I have just a little piece of a treat?" I asked, holding out my hand.

"Why, certainly, Thaddeus," she said, and broke off a corner of one, which I dropped into the jar.

"Come get a treat," I called to Lemon Drop, holding out the jar to him. It was a clean mayonnaise jar, and Lemon Drop would have to stick his tongue all the way in and smush it around to get the doggie treat out. By the time he figured out how to do it, the jar was a quarter-way full of slobber.

"Brilliant work!" Ben said in his loud voice-over whisper.

I quickly screwed a lid on the jar. The slobber inside was pretty slobbery, with crumbs of dog treat mixed in. I would have liked to get a pure sample, but sometimes you have to make compromises, even in scientific research.

Aretha volunteered to take Lemon Drop on his walk. I was going to get another sample of slobber after Lemon Drop had exercised for thirty minutes, and a last sample after we'd fed Lemon Drop ten saltine crackers. Now that I knew the trick to getting Lemon Drop to slobber in a jar, it was all going to be a piece of cake. Sure enough, at the end of the afternoon I had three labeled jars full of slobber, ready to be examined under a microscope and tested for gooeyness and

stretchiness and all sorts of other interesting characteristics.

After Aretha's mom picked her up
from Mrs. McClosky's house, Ben helped
me carry the jars to my house. "I think
I got some great footage today," he said.
"Especially when Aretha dropped Lemon
Drop's leash and had to chase him into
the pond."

When we got to my house, Ben
handed me the jars. "Okay, now remember, meet me at nine tomorrow morning
at the park behind my apartment building. Bring plenty of jars. I'll supply the
doggie treats."

I spent three hours that night experi-
menting with Lemon Drop's slobber. It
was fascinating. I thought maybe I'd
devote my life to the study of dog saliva,
it was that interesting to me. I dipped

Popsicle sticks into each jar, measuring how far each slobber sample stretched (the exercise sample stretched the farthest). I used my mom's food scale to see how much each sample weighed. I studied a sample from each jar under my microscope to see which one had the most stuff in it, which sample was the clearest, and which one was the cloudiest. I also examined each sample to see which one was just out-and-out grossest.

Definitely the cracker sample.

I have to say now, it was one of the most satisfying episodes in my scientific career.

I had no idea that by the following afternoon I'd never want to see another jar of slobber as long as I lived.

✎ chapter eight

"I do not have a good feeling about this, Mac."

Aretha and I stood at Ben's front door, each of us carrying plastic bags filled with jars, ready to do some serious dog duty. We both were wearing old jeans and T-shirts.

What we were about to do was going to involve more slobber than we ever knew existed.

Aretha leaned toward me in a confidential way. "I don't even like dogs that much. I am more of a cat person."

"So why are you doing this?" I asked her. I mean, someone like Aretha Timmons must have had a thousand other things she could be doing on a Saturday morning.

Aretha straightened up. "The badge, Mac. It's all about the badge."

Ben answered the door dressed in a camouflage jacket and sunglasses. "I hope you're ready for business," he said. He picked up his camera and a box of dog biscuits and closed the door behind him. "First up, Mrs. Klausenheimer."

Ben's mom is the manager of an apartment building where mostly old people live. Which means Ben is living in a situation where it's like he has forty extra

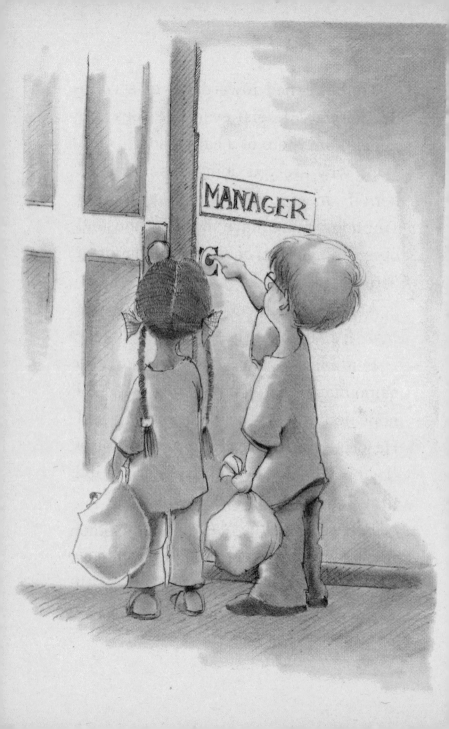

grandparents. They're always slipping sugar-free candy into his pockets and pinching his cheeks. And a bunch of them, it turns out, have dogs.

"There are a lot of miniature poodles and Chihuahuas here," Ben told us as he led us to apartment 2-D. "But Mrs. Klausenheimer has a German shepherd, and Mrs. Leonard has a bulldog, and Mr. Torres's dog is a mix of bassett hound and English sheepdog. So I think we're going to see some interesting slobber today."

I have to admit I was pretty nervous about trying to get a saliva sample from a German shepherd. Most of the dogs I've known in my lifetime besides Lemon Drop have been on the small side. Bigger than loaves of bread, smaller than tricycles. I am mostly used to dogs you don't have to be afraid of because if they started to attack you, you could run away from them, no problem.

A German shepherd is another story.

You could probably get two feet away from a German shepherd before it ate you like a prelunchtime snack.

"Benny, is that you?" Mrs. Klausenheimer called out after Ben rang her doorbell. "I've been expecting you and your little friends," she said as she opened her door. "I made brownies, no nuts."

The idea that there were brownies without nuts inside calmed me down right away. Since I am allergic to nuts, I am always missing out on treats that people's moms bring to school for special events. So you won't be surprised that Mrs. Klausenheimer automatically became one of my favorite people.

That is, until the barking started.

"Killer! Quiet down, now! It's just Benny and his little friends."

I got a shaky feeling in my knees. "Killer?"

I don't know who started backing away from the door faster, me or Aretha.

Mrs. Klausenheimer smiled. "He's not really a killer, dear. Why, he's Mommy's sweetum-peetums, that's what he is. I named him Killer to scare away the ax murderers."

She turned around and whistled. "Come here, my sweetie pie face, and show these children what a softy-wofty you are."

Killer galloped to the front door and stuck his head out.

He did not look like a sweetie pie face to me.

He looked like a dog with more teeth than were absolutely necessary.

"Now, you children come inside and we'll see if we can't get Killer to salivate for you. He's not the most—what was your word for it, Benny?"

Ben put his camera up to his eye and began recording. "Slobbery. He's not a real slobbery dog. But I bet if we give him a dog biscuit, he'll work up some slobber, won't ya, Killer?"

Killer made a noise between a bark and a growl before turning around and heading down a hallway. Everybody followed him into Mrs. Klausenheimer's living room.

"Okay, Mac, you get a biscuit out of the box, and Aretha, you get a jar ready," Ben said, handing me the doggie treats, aiming the camcorder at Killer.

That's when I made an important discovery. The scariest German shepherd in the world will be your friend if you just give him one dog biscuit.

I mean, like, your best friend for life.

I mean, when I held up the biscuit and said in pretty much a half whisper, "Here's a doggie biscuit, Killer," he knocked me to the floor, sat on me while he inhaled it in about two seconds, and then started licking me all over my face.

"Oh, Killer likes you, I can tell," Mrs. Klausenheimer said. I didn't say anything back. I was too busy getting licked to death.

"Quick, Aretha, hand Mac a jar!" Ben said, coming in closer with his camera to where I was sprawled on Mrs. Klausenheimer's scratchy rug. Aretha, who clearly was not going to get any closer to Killer than she had to, rolled a jar across the floor to me.

Getting Killer's slobber into the jar was not a problem.

Getting Killer off of me was.

I was really hoping the next dog we gathered a sample from would be a Chihuahua.

One thing we definitely learned that afternoon is a lot of dogs aren't that slobbery at all. Chihuahuas will give you a teaspoon of slobber if you're lucky. Miniature poodles, same thing.

A dog that's part bassett hound, part sheepdog, on the other hand, well, let's just say bring out the buckets, because it's about to rain saliva.

"Sheila here is a drooler," Mr. Torres told us first thing. "I think it's the bassett hound in her, isn't it, girl?" Mr. Torres leaned down and scratched Sheila behind her ears. A long string of slobber immediately started running down her chin.

"Does she do that every time you scratch her ears?" Aretha asked, sounding half fascinated and half disgusted.

Mr. Torres nodded proudly. "Just about. If there was a drooling contest, my Sheila would win it."

We filled four jars with Sheila's slobber.

We didn't need four jars, but once you figure out you can make a dog drool buckets of slobber just by scratching behind her ears, it's hard to stop.

After Sheila, me and Aretha were pretty much slobbered out. We'd gotten saliva samples from thirteen dogs. Our T-shirts and jeans were soaking wet. We had started smelling sort of bad after dog number seven, a golden retriever named Chucky. The skin on our fingers was all wrinkly.

It was time to go home.

"You should do a comic book about slobber," I told Ben as we walked back to his apartment. "Like, 'Derek the Destroyer Battles the People from Planet Slobber.'"

"I'm thinking about giving up comic

books," Ben said. He held up his camcorder and gave it a couple pats like it was his trusty sidekick. "There's a lot more future in making documentaries. That's what my dad told me when I talked to him on the phone last night."

"Documentary films are very popular right now," Aretha agreed.

Ben give up comic books? I stared at him. "Why can't you do both?"

Ben scuffed the toe of his tennis shoe against the pavement. "Well, I guess I could. But I was telling my dad about this movie that we're doing, and he sort of said that there was a really good private school near where he lives in Seattle. I might be able to get a scholarship there if I could make a brilliant documentary. They like it when kids do creative projects that use technology.

So I probably should just focus on the documentary right now."

Ben's dad lives in Seattle, Washington, which is pretty much on the other side of the country. Ben doesn't get to see his dad very much, since they live so far apart from each other. If Ben went to private school in Seattle, he'd get to see his dad all the time.

But if Ben went to private school in Seattle, I'd probably never see him again.

And if Ben lived near his dad, he'd probably never draw another comic book, just to make his dad happy.

But I was pretty sure it would make Ben miserable.

chapter nine

My teacher, Mrs. Tuttle, is very big on making lists. She says lists help to organize your mind, keep you on track, and help you not to forget things that are important to you. She says it is funny how we forget important things, but that's just the way the human brain is. There is a lot going on in there, and some stuff gets lost in the shuffle.

Last night I woke up at 2:23 a.m.,

according to my alarm clock, and had this thought: *Make a list first thing in the morning.*

It was like my brain had sent me an instant message.

What kind of list? I wondered.

And then I fell back to sleep.

This morning I woke up seven minutes and thirteen seconds early, without even trying. It was exactly enough time to make a list.

And I knew what kind of list I had to make.

A Remember What Things Are Important Right Now list.

So far this is what I have:

1. Do not let Ben move to Seattle.
2. Do not let Ben stop drawing comic books.

3. On the other hand, do not stop Ben from being his genius artistic self and doing good work on our Lemon Drop documentary and scientific experiments.
4. Do get another job so I can go to Space Camp.

I had been avoiding number four for two weeks, but now I had to face the facts: I was making thirty dollars a week walking Lemon Drop. One hundred twenty dollars a month. Times that by five months and I would have six hundred dollars.

In other words, not enough to go to Space Camp.

Even if the Lemon Drop documentary was great, we probably weren't going to sell it. Probably the best we could hope for was to show it at a school assembly. Maybe people could make donations afterward.

That still wasn't going to get me to Space Camp.

At breakfast I tried to come up with job ideas while I ate my bagel. "If only there were something I could do at school to make money," I said through a mouthful of cream cheese. "Like, I could help first graders with math or something. I could be a kind of substitute teacher."

"You're pretty good friends with the janitor," Lyle pointed out. "Maybe he's got a job you could do."

That was Lyle's first Number One Excellent Idea of the morning.

The second one came about five seconds later.

"Or maybe you could get a scholarship

to camp." Lyle took a sip of his coffee.
"I think some camps have scholarships for
kids who don't have enough money to go.
I'm not sure if technically you'd qualify,
but it's worth looking into."

I jumped out of my seat. "A scholarship!
Of course! Why didn't I think of that?"

Lyle shrugged modestly. "It *is* a pretty good idea."

I turned to my mom. "Could I please go on the Internet right now and see if they have scholarships to Space Camp?"

As you might guess, going on the Internet before school is not exactly encouraged at my house.

In fact, it's not even allowed.

"Just this once, Mom?" I begged. "If I can get a scholarship to Space Camp, then all I have to do is come up with the money for the airplane ticket. And I'll make that walking Lemon Drop."

"Mac, you know the rules," my mom said, packing up her briefcase. "If I let you go online this morning, then you'll ask to do it tomorrow morning. And if I say no tomorrow morning, you'll say, 'But you let me do it yesterday.' And do you remember what happened last time I let you use the Internet before school?"

I poked at my bagel with my finger. "I missed the bus," I mumbled.

"I'm sorry, I couldn't hear you."

"I missed the bus," I said a little more loudly. "But that was last year. This year (a) I am much more mature, and (b) I have a specific task. I just want to look up about scholarships."

My mom sighed and shook her head. I could tell she sort of wanted to give in, but she was fighting against that urge. This was a dangerous situation. If I pushed too hard, she might ban me from going online for a month, just for driving her crazy. But there was a tiny crack of opportunity here, I could see it. If I could just figure out the best approach . . .

And then something amazing happened.

Lyle stepped in.

My mom and Lyle got married four years ago, when I was five. To be honest, I didn't really understand what was going on. In fact, I was kind of scared that I would never see my real dad again, like maybe Lyle was a replacement dad.

I think that's one reason my real dad came to my mom and Lyle's wedding. Just so I would understand he wasn't going to be replaced by anybody.

In the four years that my mom and Lyle have been married, Lyle has pretty much let my mom make the rules. He'll tell me to do my chores or finish my homework, but when it comes to whether or not I can do stuff like use the computer or watch TV, he stays out of it.

But this morning he actually did something.

He said, "I've already got my computer on. How about I print out the info Mac needs?"

A simple solution to a simple problem.

My mom thought about this for a minute, probably going over her internal list of rules to make sure Lyle's using the Internet to help me out on a school morning didn't break some important law handed down from the commanders of the universe.

Then she said, "That sounds good to me. How's that sound to you, Mac?"

"That would be great," I told her, even though a part of me hated the idea of being so close to getting on the Internet and yet so far away. "Thanks, Lyle."

"Not a prob," Lyle said, and gave me a wink.

Sometimes I think Lyle understands a lot more about being a nine-year-old boy than my mom does.

While Lyle went to print out Space Camp scholarship information, I went upstairs to get dressed. I tried to remind myself not to get too excited. Even if Space Camp did give out scholarships, I might not get one.

I decided I better go ahead and talk to Mr. Reid about getting a job.

Mr. Reid is the janitor of Woodbrook Elementary. Everyone knows, though, that he really should be principal. He is pretty much a genius at everything, including automotive repairs, any kind of fix-it-up job, and slime mold identification. On top of that, all the kids like him.

It's not that the kids don't like Principal Patino. We just don't want to hang out with her in her office and get her opinion on how to improve our kickball games.

"Well, Mac, I don't have any work around here for you to do," Mr. Reid told me that afternoon in his basement office, after I'd explained that I needed a job and I needed it fast if I was ever going to make it to Space Camp. "Actually, that's not true. I just can't hire you to do the work I need done. I'm not the one who hires folks around here, the school superintendent does."

"Do you think he could hire me to do some odd jobs around the school?" I asked. "You know, sweeping, erasing chalkboards, searching out and identifying molds?"

"Doesn't work that way, Mac," Mr. Reid said. "Which is too bad, because I could use some help."

Then Mr. Reid got an idea. I could tell he'd gotten an idea because he suddenly had a sort of wondering expression on his face. Then he tapped his chin with his finger and said, "Hmmmm."

"What? Did you think of a way the superintendent could hire me?" I asked.

"No, that's not it," Mr. Reid said. "But the thought crossed my mind, I could use your help on weekends. My son, Carl, and I have started a part-time business, small building projects mostly, but we also clean out folks' garages for them, haul out their junk, that kind of thing. We were just talking last weekend that we could use another person on the team. Just to do the little jobs, breaking down boxes to recycle, sweeping up, that sort of thing."

"I'm that person, Mr. Reid," I told him. "I'd do a great job."

Mr. Reid nodded. "I know you would, Mac. The only thing is I'd need your mom and dad's permission for you to help, and one of them would need to drive you over to the job every Saturday."

"No problem," I told him. "They know how important Space Camp is to me."

Mr. Reid's beeper beeped. He looked at it and said, "Trouble up in the kinder-garten wing. I'd better get a move on." Before he left, he wrote his phone number on a piece of paper. "You have your mom or dad call me tonight so we can discuss the details."

"Okay," I said, following him out the door.

"By the way, Mac, do you know a boy named Corey Anderson? Fifth grader?"

Of course I know Corey Anderson. Everybody does. He is a famous fifth-grade scientist who won first place in both his fourth- and fifth-grade science fairs. For the fifth-grade science fair he built a computer that actually talked.

"Well, if I've got my facts straight, Corey Anderson went to Space Camp last summer. He's quite the young astronomer. You ought to talk to him about what it was like. He probably has all sorts of interesting stories he could tell you."

That sounded like a great idea. Except for the fact that at Woodbrook Elementary School fourth graders don't even think about talking to fifth-grade scientific geniuses like Corey Anderson. It just isn't done.

Mr. Reid waved as he turned the corner to the kindergarten wing. "I'll tell him you'd like to have a word with him the next time I see him."

"Thanks," I called after him. But to be honest, I just couldn't imagine it. Why would Corey Anderson ever believe that some fourth-grade kid was worth talking to, even if that kid was a scientific genius?

In my experience, fifth graders think they're the only geniuses on the planet.

🌸 chapter ten

The good news about Space Camp scholarships: They had one for academically really smart kids.

That would be me.

The bad news: I would have to write an essay to get one.

It's not that I'm a bad writer. I'm actually a pretty okay writer.

But I hate writing essays.

First of all, you are almost always

given a topic you don't have any interest in. Then you have to write an outline that shows you will:

I. Introduce your topic in a brilliant way
II. Have a brilliant first point (you will need a topic sentence)
III. Have a brilliant second point (another topic sentence goes here)
IV. Have a brilliant third point (come up with yet another stupid topic sentence)
V. Conclude your essay in a brilliant way (restating all topic sentences using different words, even though it was hard enough coming up with the words for the first time)

Then you have to hand your essay in and have Mrs. Tuttle write all over it in purple ink, which, if you're me, will give you hives.

All in all, it is not a very fun process.

Mostly what I don't like about writing essays is that you never get to write about stuff that's interesting. The last essay we had to write for language arts was on the topic of cafeteria food—was it nutritious enough? First of all, I am not a nutritionist, so I am not qualified to comment on the nutritional value of cafeteria food. Second of all, I don't care if it's nutritious or not. If they have pizza and french fries on the days I buy lunch, that's all that's important.

I was thinking about all of this on my way to my dad's house on Friday afternoon after school. My mom was driving me. When I asked her what she thought I should write about for my scholarship essay, she said she thought I should write about the importance of space travel or how Space Camp would change my life.

I knew those were pretty okay topics. The only thing was I also knew every other kid was going to write on the exact same thing. If my essay was the last one the scholarship people read, they'd be so bored of reading about the importance of space travel, they'd automatically throw my essay in the trash.

To be honest, I wouldn't blame them.

I was hoping a weekend at my dad's house would kick-start the part of my brain responsible for coming up with scholarship-winning essay topics. That would make up for the fact that I was going to miss what would have been my first day on the job with Mr. Reid. He and my mom agreed that I could work four hours every Saturday afternoon, for five dollars an hour.

If you added that twenty dollars a weekend to the thirty dollars a week I made walking Lemon Drop, that was fifty dollars a week, or two hundred dollars a month.

It would be just enough to get me to Space Camp, if I didn't get sick or break an arm.

Or take weekends off.

Don't get me wrong. I love going to my dad's house. First of all, he has a flat-screen TV, and on Friday nights we watch old-time movies on it, like Abbott and Costello and the Three Stooges. It's just this guy thing we do.

Second, my dad is, like, the world's greatest math teacher, so we spend a lot of time testing out math games and puzzles for him to use when he teaches. I always leave my dad's house feeling like my brain has been sharpened.

Third, my dad doesn't recycle. Now, I am for the environment and not against recycling. I think it's good that my mom recycles everything that has an atom of recyclable material in it. But sometimes it's kind of fun to throw something away. Just chuck it into the trash can without a second thought.

Do not tell my mom I said that.

I was prepared to spend the whole two-hour drive worrying about my essay topic and how I was going to make enough money for Space Camp if I didn't win the scholarship, when my mom turned on the radio. The newscaster was talking about Mars.

It turns out that a little bit of Mars news will cheer me up in no time flat.

"And now, here's the latest on what's been happening on Mars," the announcer said, sounding like he'd done the research himself instead of just reading it off of a piece of paper. "Looks like Mars is wetter than we thought. NASA's *Spirit* rover has been kicking up Mars's dirt and getting the dirt on it. A recent discovery shows that there's plenty of silica on the red planet, and as we all

know, the production of silica requires water. A NASA spokesperson called this 'a remarkable discovery.'"

"Did you hear that, Mom?" I leaned forward and pounded on the back of her seat. "Water on Mars! Water means life! There's life on Mars!"

"But is there takeout?" my mom asked, cracking herself up.

"Mom, this is serious. If there's water on Mars, humans can live on Mars."

"But there aren't any trees on Mars, no flowers or birds," my mom pointed out. "Who wants to live on a planet without trees or flowers or birds?"

My mom is such a mom, it's ridiculous.

However, her comment did give me a great idea. If Mars had water, why couldn't you grow things on it? There were weather issues to deal with, of course, lots of space radiation, for one thing, and meteor showers, and it was cold—like, below-zero-in-the-middle-of-summer cold. But scientists think that with the right equipment and protective gear, astronauts will be able to go to Mars one day, and one day people might actually be able to live there. So why not build the first Martian greenhouse and grow the first Martian tomatoes?

Because the fact is I really love tomato sandwiches.

I told my dad my great idea the minute I saw him.

"I think you might be onto something, Mac," he said, taking out a carton of ice cream from his freezer. That is our ritual: We wave good-bye to my mom, watch her pull the minivan out of the driveway, then head inside my dad's house to make milk shakes.

He dumped practically the whole half gallon into the blender and poured in some milk. "The thing is you've got to deal with the fact that the air is pretty thin on Mars. You'd have to research how plants could survive with so little oxygen. Or how to create an oxygenated environment for them."

"Like a greenhouse?" I asked, pushing the mix button on the blender.

"Yeah, I guess it would be something like that. But maybe sturdier than a greenhouse you'd have on Earth. More protective. Mars has a pretty harsh environment."

A few minutes later we were sitting on the couch, drinking our milk shakes and watching a golf tournament on TV.

Watching televised golf is pretty much my dad's main flaw.

Letting me drink milk shakes on the couch makes up for it, though.

I was getting a relaxed feeling from drinking milk shakes and hanging out on my dad's couch, which is a hundred percent comfortable. Also, I was just sort of happy. My brain was filled with good, scientific thoughts.

Then I remembered to ask my dad what he thought I should write about for the Space Camp scholarship essay.

My dad looked at me and grinned. "Uh, duh? What did we discuss as soon as you walked in the door, Einstein?"

I was so relaxed, I couldn't remember. We'd talked about a hundred things since I walked in the door. "What flavor ice cream to make milk shakes with?"

My dad slapped his forehead. "Mac, Mac, Mac! Don't make me spell it out for you, buddy. Think about it—what were we just discussing *while* we made milk shakes?"

"Tomatoes?"

My dad nodded. "Exactly. Tomatoes."

I shook my head.

Tomatoes.

It was that simple.

☆ chapter eleven

"'How to Make a Tomato Sandwich on Mars'?"

Aretha shook her head and bounced her pencil a couple of times, then started reading the essay I'd just handed her. I waited nervously to hear what she thought.

I thought it was a work of genius, but that didn't mean Aretha would.

Scientists sometimes have very different opinions on controversial topics.

I had gotten my entire essay written by World Studies period, right before lunch. I wrote about building greenhouses on Mars, and how I was going to be the first tomato grower on the red planet, which was kind of cool, since tomatoes were red too. I talked about the weather on Mars, and the possibility human beings could actually live on Mars one day and grow food there. It would be hard work and would take a long time, I concluded, but I believed that one day earthlings would be happily eating tomato sand-wiches and many other tomato products in a restaurant on the next planet over.

It is the first essay I have ever really, truly been excited about writing.

I mean, in my life.

Aretha took forever to read it. She bounced her pencil while she read. I couldn't tell if she was excited to read it or was just coming up with a bunch of critical things to say about it.

Aretha is a big believer in constructive criticism.

Emphasis on the "criticism" part of that phrase.

Finally she leaned forward and handed my essay back to me. She had a thoughtful expression on her face, like she was trying to find the exact right words to express herself. After about a million years she said, "Not bad, Mac. In fact, I'd call it interesting and thought-provoking. I bet nobody else writes about tomato sandwiches."

"That's what I'm counting on," I told her.

I felt great for the rest of the day. If Aretha liked my essay, then the Space

Camp scholarship judges would probably love it. I could take the money I earned from walking Lemon Drop and working for Mr. Reid and use it all to buy a round-trip plane ticket. Any leftover money I could use for the chemistry set I'd been saving up for since third grade.

Ben rode home on the bus with me that afternoon. We were going to do some more slobber work. Correction: I was going to do slobber work. Ben was going to document me doing slobber work.

"Guess what I just heard?" Ben asked as the bus pulled out of the Woodbrook Elementary School parking lot. "You won't believe it."

"They're finally going to make Mr. Reid principal?"

Ben grinned. "I wish. But it's even cooler than that. I heard some slobber news."

"Slobber news? Like, on the Slobber News Channel?"

The Slobber News Channel.

Sometimes I crack myself up.

"Har, har, very funny, Mac." Ben smacked my knee with his spelling book to let me know just how funny he thought I was. "No, I heard it from Chester Oliphant. He was going to share it at Share and Stare, but we ran out of time."

Chester Oliphant is the funniest boy in our class. In fact, he is so funny that I haven't mentioned our slobber experiments to him. I have a feeling I would be hearing a lot of slobber jokes if I did. He is a pretty nice person, so they wouldn't be mean jokes, but my guess is there would be a lot of them.

For, like, the next five years.

"So, what slobber news did Chester have?" I asked.

"Gila monster slobber," Ben announced. He leaned back in his seat and smiled. "How coolazoid is that? You know what a Gila monster is, right? It's a kind of lizard. It's not a real monster or anything."

I sighed. "I'm pretty sure I knew that already, Ben."

Ben shrugged. "You never know. Anyway, scientists are using Gila monster slobber for medicine. For people with diabetes."

"That's really cool," I admitted. "That's like what we found out about vampire bats online. How their saliva might be good for people with heart problems."

"I'd probably have a heart attack if someone tried to give me vampire slobber," Ben said. "So I don't think it would be very good for *me*."

"But just think: Gila monsters, vampire bats . . . it's like all this saliva is good for you. And don't forget that dog slobber might be good for you too." I was starting to get excited. "The saliva research we're doing could be the next big thing."

"I guess," Ben said. "I mean, don't get me wrong. I think it's great research. Only, exactly what are we discovering?"

I had to think a minute. "Well, we know that Labrador retrievers and bassett hounds have the gooiest slobber, and that Chihuahuas have the wateriest."

"Yeah, but what does that prove?"

The bus pulled up to my stop. Ben and I got off, only Ben got off like a person in a normal mood, and when I stepped on the sidewalk, I was totally depressed.

My slobber experiments didn't prove anything.

By the time we got to my room, I was ready to give up slobber science altogether. What could a fourth-grade scientist add to the amazing findings grown-up scientists had already come up with?

I was pretty sure the answer to that was "Nothing."

"Look at it this way, Mac," Ben said, flopping down on my floor and searching for a snack under my bed. "It's pretty neat that you came up with the idea of slobber research on your own."

"Didn't you come up with the idea?" I asked him. I grabbed a bag of cheese crackers from my top desk drawer and tossed them to Ben.

"No, I'm pretty sure you did," he said, opening up the bag of crackers and inhaling them. "At least, I think you did. Anyway, you were the one who got the idea to look up dog slobber online."

Ben sat up. He popped the last of the crackers in his mouth. And then his mouth fell wide open. I could see a bunch of chewed-up crackers inside.

Which was pretty gross, in case you were wondering.

Ben pointed to the top of my dresser, where all of the jars of dog slobber were sitting. He swallowed. "Um, is it my imagination, or is there something growing in some of those jars?"

We both got up to look. Sure enough, mold was growing in five of the jars. I checked out the labels. The slobber belonged to Lemon Drop and Sheila, the dogs with the thickest saliva samples.

There was no mold growing in the jars collected from the Chihuahuas, miniature poodles, or Killer.

"I don't know what it proves," I told Ben. "But it proves something."

Ben nodded. "We might just be on to some amazing discovery here."

"Yep," I said. "We just have to figure out what."

chapter twelve

I have noticed that my life can go for long stretches without anything happening at all. I go to school, I come home and do my homework, I watch TV for thirty minutes, I play on the computer for thirty minutes, and at nine o'clock I go to bed.

It sounds more boring than it actually is.

I mean, don't forget that there is a

bunch of eating, too, plus hanging out with Ben and walking Lemon Drop.

And there is my dried worm collecting. As of three weeks ago I am up to 178 dried worms. I mean, in pristine condition, no broken or partial ones.

I'm pretty sure that is a world record.

But here is what always happens: Just when my life is going at a slow, steady pace, events start piling on top of one another until it seems like everything is happening at once.

There is a scientific explanation for this.

I just don't know what it is.

Here is everything that has happened in the last five days, starting with Saturday.

The first thing that happened was I went to work for Mr. Reid. Correction: Lyle and I went to work for Mr. Reid.

Lyle was just supposed to drop me off on his way to Fitness World. But when we got to the house Mr. Reid and his son, Carl, were working at, 4356 Brightwood Way, he decided he should give Mr. Reid his cell phone number, just in case there was an accident or we got finished early. And then he got interested in what Mr. Reid was doing when we found him, which was tearing the deck off the back of the house. Mr. Reid said they were going to replace it with a screened porch.

"Boy, I used to do this kind of work during the summers when I was in college," Lyle told Mr. Reid. I could see him looking at the crowbar in Mr. Reid's hand. His eyes got all shiny, like he wouldn't mind taking a whack at something himself.

Mr. Reid noticed too. He handed Lyle

the crowbar. "Have at it. I need a few minutes to show Mac what to do."

We left Lyle trying to pry off a railing from the side of the deck. He was pulling at it and twisting around and getting all red in the face.

It was the happiest I've ever seen him.

Mr. Reid pulled a pair of work gloves from his overalls pocket and handed them to me. "Your job is going to be moving pieces of the deck from here," he said, pointing to a pile of pried-off deck pieces, "to there." He pointed to a humongous portable Dumpster. "Watch out for nails, okay?"

I nodded. Then Mr. Reid led me to the garage, where a man was sawing some boards. "This is my son, Carl," he said. "Carl, this is Mac."

Carl waved at me. "Glad to have you

on board, Mac. Dad tells me you're quite the scientist. I hear you're going to Space Camp."

"If I can save up enough money," I told him.

"Well, good luck," he said. "I was always interested in space. When I was a kid, I thought I might be an astronaut one day. Saved up all my money to buy a telescope. Boy, I used to spend half the night looking through that thing. It's still up in Dad's attic, as a matter of fact. It's pretty beat up, but if you wanted to try it out, I'd be happy to lend it to you. But you probably already have one, huh?"

I shook my head. Why hadn't it occurred to me to get a telescope? I could be studying the planets every night from

my backyard. I could be making important astronomical discoveries. I could
be spying on our next-door neighbor Mr.
Clutterman, who seemed very nice but
sort of nervous, like he had a secret he
was trying to hide out in his garage. . . .

Not that I would ever use a scientific
instrument for something as unscientific
as spying.

Nope, not me.

"You don't have a telescope?" Carl asked.
"Then I'll bring my old one next—"

He was interrupted by a huge crash.
We all ran out to the yard, where we
found Lyle standing in the middle
of a pile of boards, grinning.

"I finished the job myself,"
he said. "Mind if I hang
around and help out
some more?"

That is how Lyle became the fourth employee of Reid & Son, Inc.

The next thing that happened was that on Monday I met Corey Anderson, Genius Fifth-Grade Scientist.

It wasn't by choice. Mr. Reid stopped by Mrs. Tuttle's classroom first thing in the morning and told me to come by his office when I was done eating lunch. Corey would be there, waiting to talk to me about Space Camp.

For the rest of the morning I was as jumpy as an overheated atom.

"Why are you making such a big deal about this guy?" Ben asked me at lunch. "He's just another human being, like you or me."

"I know, but I want to make a good impression." I finished chewing my tuna fish sandwich. "The thing with fifth graders is, they think they're such a big deal. And Corey Anderson sort of is a big deal. I mean, he's pretty much a certified scientific genius. But I want him to know that I'm not a nobody."

"You want me to go with you?" Ben asked. He flexed his arms to show off his muscles and cracked his knuckles. "In case this Corey Anderson kid needs some straightening out?"

I shook my head. I appreciated that Ben wanted to stick up for me, but I was pretty sure things wouldn't get violent. I just didn't want to walk out of the room feeling like a failure. What if Corey Anderson told me he didn't think I was Space Camp material? What if he doubted my scientific credentials? I mean, what did I have to show for myself, except for an honorable-mention ribbon from the fourth-grade science fair and an excellent collection of slime mold?

As it turned out, the slime mold was all I needed.

That's pretty much always the case.

"Slime mold rocks," Corey told me two seconds after Mr. Reid introduced us. We were in Mr. Reid's office, just kicking back like a couple of Einsteins who'd finished lunch early. "Mr. Reid told me all about your collection. You're so lucky your house is near some woods. There's maybe two trees in my yard. I've looked everywhere for slime mold, but it's not to be found."

"Does your house have a crawl space?" I asked him.

He nodded.

"You should try under there. Crawl

spaces can get pretty damp. There's not a lot of light, and slime mold likes a little light, but still, I found a pretty good sample of *Physarum* once in our crawl space."

Corey Anderson's eyes grew wide. "No way! That's so cool."

Then we got down to business.

"Here's the thing about Space Camp," Corey said, leaning back in his chair. "It's the most awesome thing you'll ever experience."

"What was your favorite part?" I asked.

"That's easy," Corey said, grinning. "The Mars roller coaster."

I nearly fell out of my chair. "A roller coaster? On Mars?"

Corey sat up and pointed toward the ceiling. "You know how Mars has humongous mountains?"

I nodded, looking up, like I could see the mountains on Mars from where I was sitting.

"Well, basically, on the Mars roller coaster you're getting a feel for what it would be like to ride down one of those mountains. And you go reeeaaaallly fast. One kid threw up."

"Cool!" I said.

Corey looked sort of embarrassed. "Actually, it was me," he admitted. "But it was really close to the end. And up to that point I was having a great time."

"It sounds awesome," I told him.

"Did I mention you get to build your own rocket—and launch it?" Corey asked. "You would not believe how high up those things go."

I fell back in my chair.

I'd read about the rocket launches, but that wasn't the same as someone talking about them in real life. The idea that I might launch my own rocket was almost too much for me. I have been asking my mom for a rocket launcher kit since I was five. She says I can have one when I'm thirty.

But if I went to Space Camp, I would launch my first rocket before I even turned ten.

At that point it was official: I was going to Space Camp if I had to sell everything I owned to get there. Even my slime mold collection.

Okay, maybe not my slime mold collection.

But I'd trade my dried worm collection for a week at Space Camp.

And that's saying something.

• • •

The third thing that happened: Ben finished the Lemon Drop documentary.

Here's what I'd been counting on: that he'd never finish it. Ben is the sort of person who has a lot of unfinished projects lying around. I think it's because he's very creative and is always coming up with new ideas. He'll be working on one comic book when an idea for another one will come to him, so he'll start working on a second comic book.

He always finishes his comic books eventually, but it can take months of going back and forth between "Derek the Destroyer Versus the Mutant Toad Warriors," "Derek the Destroyer Versus the Putrid Pea Men," and "Derek the Destroyer Versus the United Ignited Iguanas."

So I figured the same thing would

happen with the Lemon Drop documentary. Which would solve my problem of Ben applying to private school near where his dad lived, because, let's face it, a stack of comic books he'd drawn, no matter how amazing they were, wasn't going to get him accepted anywhere.

So when he walked into Mrs. Tuttle's room Wednesday morning waving a USB memory stick at me, I went cold all over.

"It's all right here, Mac!" he shouted across the room. "My brilliantoid Lemon Drop documentary, uploaded fresh from my camcorder this morning. We can watch it on Mr. Reid's computer at lunchtime."

My only hope was that Ben's Lemon Drop documentary would be terrible. But I couldn't *really* hope that, because I knew Ben had worked hard on it. It was important to him. And I knew that he hoped it would make a good impression on his dad.

So when *Lemon Drop: Dog Slobberer* turned out to be brilliant, I did my best to feel happy for him.

But I felt terrible. I knew I was about to lose my best friend. Which, in case you were wondering, is one of the worst feelings in the world you can have. Especially when you know you'll never have another best friend as good as the one you have now.

"So when's the application due, anyway?" I asked him as we got back to Mrs. Tuttle's classroom. I was thinking about the great scene where the camera caught Lemon Drop batting his slobbery tennis ball against the garage door with his paw. "He's playing slobberball!" Ben had yelled, and Lemon Drop turned to the camera and started barking, like he couldn't believe that Ben figured out what he was doing. Then he whacked the ball so hard against the garage door that it bounced about ten feet into the air. Lemon Drop caught it in his mouth and started turning around in circles on his hind legs.

How could any school not accept Ben after seeing that?

"What application?"

"For that private school near your dad's house," I told him. "The one you're going to try to get a scholarship to?"

"Oh, that's not until

high school," Ben said. "I just wanted to get an early start learning how to make documentaries. By high school I'm going to be like George Lucas or somebody, don't you think?"

High school?

He wasn't going to apply to private school in Seattle until high school?

That was about a hundred years away.

I didn't know whether to laugh or sock him in the nose.

"George Lucas doesn't make documentaries, bozo," I told him. I decided I was too relieved to do anything but call him a dumb name.

Ben turned and looked at me. "*Star Wars* isn't a documentary?"

"It's all made up," I informed him. "Luke Skywalker, Darth Vader—they never existed."

Ben looked shocked.

And then he nearly fell on the ground laughing.

Mrs. Tuttle came over to see what the problem was. She ended up throwing one of the rubber frogs she keeps in a jar on her desk at him. Not hard, just enough to get his attention.

Ben stood up and wiped tears from his eyes. "I guess *E.T.: The Extra-Terrestrial* isn't a documentary either, huh?"

I froze. *E.T.* wasn't for real?

I'd always sort of thought it was.

chapter thirteen

On Wednesday I got two dozen petri dishes in the mail.

It was like a dream come true.

"Mrs. Cavazos, the ninth-grade biology teacher, was cleaning out her supply closet," my dad told me when I called him to say thanks. "She had some extras she couldn't use and remembered I had a son who was a budding biologist, so she gave them to me."

Strictly speaking, I prefer not to limit myself to one branch of the sciences. On the other hand, if someone gives me two dozen petri dishes because they think I'm a biologist, I'm not exactly going to tell them they're wrong.

I opened the box and took out a dish. A petri dish is a small, flat-bottomed container that comes with a lid. You can use it for all kinds of experiments, but mostly it gets used for growing stuff. You put some special petri-dish jelly in it (called nutrient agar) and then samples of stuff, like bacteria or even seeds, and see what grows.

That's what happens when the doctor thinks you have strep throat. Your tonsils get jabbed with a giant cotton swab, and then

159

the doctor rubs the cotton swab in a petri dish and waits for something to develop. If it's streptococcus bacteria, be prepared to spend the next week swallowing a bunch of putrid pink antibiotics.

Just warning you.

Anyway, after I got off the phone with my dad, I tried to think of some great experiments I could run using my new petri dishes. Growing bacteria wouldn't be too hard, since bacteria is everywhere and multiplies like crazy. All I'd have to do was prepare the nutrient agar, put it in a petri dish, and leave the dish uncovered for a little while. Plenty of bacteria would find its way in.

Or, I thought, I could use a Q-tip and do a swab of the inside of my cheek.

Or . . .

And then it came to me.

I am a genius.

I called Ben. "You need to ride the bus home with me tomorrow," I told him. "Get your mom to write a note."

"Okay," Ben said. "Any reason?"

"I'll tell you tomorrow. But it's pretty gross."

I could feel Ben grinning through the phone receiver. "Cool," he said. "Then I'll definitely be there."

The next day I brought two jars in my backpack. When me and Ben got off the bus, I held out one jar to Ben and said, "Spit, please."

Ben took a step back. "Spit? Why?"

"Just do it, okay?"

Ben shrugged. "Okay. No prob. I like to spit."

"Make it a good one," I told him.

He did. "Now, do you mind telling me what's going on?" he asked.

We started walking over to Mrs. McClosky's house. "Remember when you thought we should do an experiment to test the difference between your spit and Lemon Drop's?"

Ben nodded.

"Well, at the time I couldn't see the point," I admitted. "But on Saturday it hit me. I was thinking about how that mold was growing in Lemon Drop's slobber jar."

"And Sheila's," Ben reminded me.

"And Sheila's. So obviously some mold spores got in their jars and started growing. But what allowed the mold to grow?"

"Mold likes slobber?"

"No," I told him. "Mold likes bacteria. Spores got in the jar, and those spores were able to survive because they were feeding on the bacteria in Lemon Drop's slobber."

"And Sheila's," Ben said.

"And Sheila's. Probably because we were able to get really good samples from them."

"Okay," Ben said, "I'm following you so far. But I still don't see what this has to do with me spitting in a jar."

We were getting close to Mrs. McClosky's house. I could hear Lemon Drop barking. That's something I always like about Lemon Drop. He gets excited whenever he realizes I'm in the neighborhood.

"Remember when we first started talking about slobber, and you said you'd heard that dogs' mouths were cleaner than humans'?"

"Yeah, I remember."

"That's what we're going to find out," I told him. "Let's see whose slobber grows more bacteria."

Ben slapped me on the back, making me fall forward a few steps before I grabbed a shrub to steady myself. "Mac! You're a genius! We'll settle this question once and for all. We'll be famous!"

Unfortunately, when we got to Mrs. McClosky's house, Lemon Drop wasn't in a slobbering mood. There was only one thing to do.

We called Aretha.

Ten minutes later she showed up on her bike. "I don't understand why you need me to make Lemon Drop salivate. Just give him some water."

"What can we say? You have the slobber touch, Aretha," Ben said.

Aretha nodded. "It's true, I do an excellent job of getting dogs to drool into a jar."

"It's a gift," Ben agreed.

As soon as Lemon Drop saw Aretha, it was like he got a big smile on his face. I know dogs don't really smile, but that's really how it looked. He even stood on his hind legs and put his front paws on Aretha's shoulders so he could give her a big smooch on the nose.

"Lemon Drop, I hate to say it, but you have got some foul-smelling breath," Aretha told him.

"That's great news!" I exclaimed. "Halitosis is

an indication of a very active bacteria population."

"And I brushed my teeth this morning," Ben said. "Which I hardly ever do. But I bet that means my spit has hardly any bacteria compared to Lemon Drop's."

We took Lemon Drop on a walk around the block, and when we got back, Aretha got him to drink about a gallon of water.

We got half a jar of slobber, no problem.

When my mom got home from work that afternoon, me, Aretha, and Ben were in the kitchen cooking up some nutrient agar jelly. You do it the same way you make regular Jell-O—put the agar in a bowl, add some boiling water, and stir. Sarah P. Fortemeyer, my Teenage Baby-sitter from Outer Space, was overseeing the project.

"I hope you don't mind," Sarah told my mom after she'd explained what we were doing. "Mac said he thought it would be okay."

"Are you observing all kitchen safety rules?" my mom asked.

Ben held up a spoon. "No sharp knives, Mrs. M."

Aretha held up a pot holder. "We have protected ourselves from burns and other injuries."

My mom nodded her approval. "Good job. I'm glad to see Mac has such responsible friends."

I thought Ben was going to explode from happiness when my mom said that.

I don't think anyone has ever called him responsible before.

There is a reason for that.

• • •

When the nutrient agar had completely dissolved, we poured it carefully into four petri dishes—two for Lemon Drop's slobber, two for Ben's. We let it cool and thicken. Then, using an eyedropper, we added equal amounts of slobber to each dish.

I have never felt so scientific in my life.

"It shouldn't take long, guys," I said when we were finished. "I'd say four days tops."

"And then we will have solved the age-old mystery—whose mouth is cleaner, a human's or a dog's?" Ben said.

Aretha got a thoughtful look on her face. "I wonder if there's a badge for dental hygiene." She stood up. "I better get home and check my Girl Scout handbook," she said. "I don't want to miss out on any possible badge advancement."

After Ben and Aretha left, I carefully carried the petri dishes up to my room and put them on my desk.

Then I sat on my bed and watched them.

I knew it would take a while before the bacteria started multiplying, but I didn't care. I picked up the telescope that Carl had lent me and aimed it at the dishes. Through a telescope things up close look huge and blurry. I couldn't see a thing.

So I aimed the telescope out my window instead. Venus, the evening star, was just coming out underneath an almost invisible moon. It was a very satisfying feeling to sit there with a sky filling up with stars in front of me and petri dishes full of developing bacteria beside me. My slime mold was up on the shelves

over my desk, and my collection of the Mysteries of Planet Zindar books was under my bed.

Scientifically speaking, life does not get much better than that.

chapter fourteen

My name is Phineas L. MacGuire.

But you can call me Mission Specialist MacGuire if you want to.

In fact, I'd kind of prefer it.

It's what the guys on Team Gemini call me. Or at least it's what they'll call me when I get to Space Camp.

Which should be in two hours.

In case you were wondering, so far I haven't thrown up on the plane, even if it is my first time riding on one. I think this is good news if I'm going to be an astronaut. The fact is Corey Anderson is not the first person to have thrown up in a space-simulator situation. It happens to a lot of people.

But I really, really don't want it to happen to me.

When the plane lands, I will be picked up at the baggage carousel by Wanda J. Lupino, my mother's college roommate, whom supposedly I met once when I was three and liked a lot. My mother says that Wanda J. Lupino and I bonded immediately, whatever that means.

The important thing is I won't have to ride in a taxi to Space Camp. For some reason I got nervous every time I thought about that. It's one thing to ride in an airplane all by yourself. It's another thing to get in a taxi and try to get somewhere. What if the taxi driver had never heard of Space Camp? What if it turned out I didn't have enough money to pay him? What if he made me work at a restaurant washing dishes until I made enough money to pay him?

In my book, Wanda J. Lupino is a lifesaver.

"Now, Mac, be sure to ask the flight attendant to walk with you to the baggage claim," my mom told me as we waited for my flight to be announced. "I've already talked with the airline people, and they say that's no problem. If I know you, you'll want to find the baggage claim yourself, but please don't. Will you promise me that, honey?"

"I promise," I told her. I tried to sound annoyed, like I couldn't believe she was

175

making me do such a babyish thing. But really I didn't mind. My only goal was to get to Space Camp without getting lost.

Also, I preferred to get there without my mother having a nervous breakdown.

"Do you think you have enough money, honey?" she asked, digging through her purse for her wallet. "Because you might want to buy a souvenir T-shirt or something."

"I've got money, Mom," I assured her. "I have fifty dollars that Dad gave me."

My mom sniffled a little. "I can't believe I'm letting you fly down there all by yourself."

Lyle put his hand on her shoulder. "Mac will be fine. He's a sensible kid. And Wanda will be waiting for him. There's absolutely nothing to worry about."

"Except if the plane crashes," I pointed out.

My mom burst into tears.

Lyle sighed. "The plane isn't going to crash, Mac. Flying is perfectly safe."

"I know that," I said. "I have a better chance of having a heart attack and dying on the plane than the plane crashing. The odds are completely against it. I'm not worried at all. Besides, you fly at least four times a year, Mom. So you of all people should know how safe it is."

My mom sniffed and tried to smile. "That's right, honey, it's perfectly safe."

Fortunately my flight was announced before

my mom could think up another good reason to cry. We all did a bunch of hugging, and my mom blew her nose a couple of times, really big honker blows, and then we waved and said good-bye, just like in the movies.

It wasn't until I was walking down that little hallway that leads to the plane that I remembered something very important. I ran back to my mom and Lyle. "Do you know those petri dishes that are on my desk?" I called out.

"What about them?" my mom asked. She sounded suspicious.

"Well, they're full of bacteria, so would you mind cleaning them out and running them through the dishwasher?"

My mom's mouth fell open in a huge O. Lyle put his hand on her back to steady her. "Sure, Mac, no problem. I'll

Bacteria

take care of it tonight. Is it any kind of bacteria in particular? I mean, do I need to take any precautions?"

"It's just the kind that grows in slobber," I said as I started to turn back for the plane. "I'm pretty sure it's not dangerous. You might want to use gloves while you're disposing of it, though, just in case."

Lyle gave me a weak wave. "Great, Mac. I'll do that."

After I got on the plane and buckled in, I leaned back and thought about the bacteria growing in the Petri dishes back home. Sometimes thinking about germs can calm you down when you're feeling nervous about stuff. Mostly I was nervous about getting sick on the plane. I really didn't want to be known at Space Camp as the kid who tossed his breakfast on Flight 432. But once I started thinking about our slobber experiments, I forgot about throwing up entirely.

When the bacteria had started growing in the petri dishes six days after we'd set up the experiments, we just couldn't let it stop, even though we knew we'd have to get rid of it eventually. Bacteria isn't like slime mold. It's not like a plant you can keep around and enjoy to your heart's content.

Still, it's pretty cool when you see it growing in a petri dish on top of your desk.

The minute he heard the bacteria was growing, Ben rushed over with his camcorder. "I want to document this," he

said. "And then we can send it off to the Science Channel." He moved closer to the desk and began doing his voice-over whisper. "Ladies and gentlemen, the great genius scientist Phineas L. 'Mac' MacGuire has finally proved something that no scientist before him has ever proved."

Then he looked over at me. "Um, what exactly have you proved here, Mac?"

"Well, I can't say I've proved it definitively, but what's growing in these petri dishes certainly suggests that dogs' mouths really are cleaner than humans'. That is, if you define clean as lack of bacterial growth."

Ben went back to his voice-over. "That's right, folks. You heard it here first. Dogs have the cleanest mouths of all amphibians."

"Um, I think you mean mammals," I said.

"Right, whatever," Ben said, waving my comment away. "I'm just trying to sound scientific for our documentary."

After filming for a few more minutes, Ben put his camera down, and we sat on my bed and ate some pretzel sticks I'd found inside my pillowcase. We were discussing whether or not the experiment would have turned out different if Ben actually brushed his teeth more than four times a week, when there was a knock on my door.

When I said, "Come in," Sarah P. Fortemeyer entered. In her hand was a white envelope.

"You want to know what the return address says?" she asked, handing the envelope to me. "It says 'Space Camp.'

Actually, it says 'U.S. Space and Rocket Center.' Pretty cool, huh, Mac?"

I waited until Sarah left before opening it. "This is it, Ben," I said. "This is when we find out if I got a scholarship or not."

"I bet you did," Ben said. "I mean, who could be smarter than you?"

If you ever wondered why Ben is my best friend, even if he isn't a genius scientist, well, that's pretty much it.

I mean, your best friend should always think you're the best. I think Ben's the best artist; he thinks I'm the best scientist.

Also, neither of us minds eating pretzels that have been stuck inside my pillowcase for the last six months.

My hands were a little

shaky as I pulled the letter from the envelope and started to read it. "'Dear Phineas L. MacGuire,'" I read out loud.

"That's good news!" Ben exclaimed. "They're calling you by your name. If it started out 'To Whom It May Concern,' that would be bad. But this is really good. Keep reading!"

I kept reading. "'Because of the many strong academic scholarship applications we received this year, the Scholarship Committee has had to make some difficult decisions.'"

"That's bad news," Ben said. "When they start out saying they've had to make a difficult decision, well, that can't be good."

I glared at him. "Could you just let me read, please?"

"Yeah, yeah, read, read. What's stopping you? Go on!"

I went on. "'We have decided to award several partial scholarships this year. While we are sorry we can't offer you a full Space Camp scholarship, we hope that this partial scholarship will aid you in your efforts to attend camp this spring. Please contact our office with any questions or concerns.'"

At the bottom of the page someone had written, "Great idea about growing tomatoes on Mars. Look forward to discussing this with you at camp!"

It was signed *Gene Cernan*.

Also known as the Last Man to Walk on the Moon.

I had the personal autograph of a bona fide astronaut.

My life would never be the same again.

"Frame this letter, Mac!" Ben grabbed the letter from me and waved it around.

"It's gonna be worth, like, a million dollars someday."

I doubted it.

But I knew I'd frame the letter anyway.

After I called my mom at work to tell her about the scholarship, Ben and I went to tell Lemon Drop. Lemon Drop was an important part of my Space Camp adventure, and I felt that he should be one of the first people to hear my good news. The fact is without Lemon Drop I wouldn't even be going to Space Camp. I wouldn't have enough money to go.

We were three houses down from Mrs. McClosky's house when Lemon Drop started barking. And then he came running toward us. He had his slobberball in his mouth.

"You first," I said to Ben, pointing at the ball.

"Oh, no," Ben said. "After you. I insist."

Lemon Drop dropped the slobberball in my hand.

Guess who was going first?

Mrs. McClosky stuck her head out the door. "Gustavus, would you boys like some cookies? Lemon Drop and I made them earlier this afternoon."

Ben and I looked at each other. Lemon Drop made cookies? Could he be an even bigger genius than we had guessed?

"He did all the stirring all by himself," Mrs. McClosky said proudly. "All I had to do was put the spoon in his mouth. Oh, he's quite a remarkable dog, my Lemon Drop."

We looked at Lemon Drop slobbering all over the sidewalk.

We looked at each other again.

"No, thank you, Mrs. McClosky," we said at the same time.

Here are the facts: I am a scientist.

I am willing to go to extraordinary lengths to understand the world around me.

I am not willing to eat slobber cookies.

Not even if they are made with the slobber of a truly genius dog.

Although, it occurs to me that if dog slobber has as many beneficial properties as the research suggests, slobber cookies may actually be good for you.

I'll get back to you on that.

First I'm going to Mars.

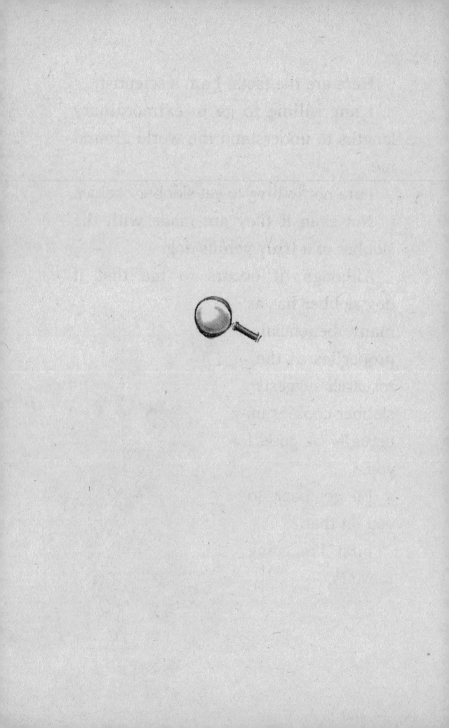

MAC'S SCIENCE EXPERIMENTS

IS THERE LIFE ON MARS?

What you'll need:

- 3 jars (mayonnaise jar-sized)
- sand
- baking powder
- salt
- yeast
- sugar water (one cup water mixed with
    a tablespoon of sugar)

How to do it:

Fill each jar halfway with sand. Put two teaspoons of
baking powder in one jar, two teaspoons of salt in
the next jar, and two teaspoons of yeast in the third
jar. Don't forget to label the jars! Refrigerate the
jars overnight, so they get cold like Mars.

The next day add warm sugar water to each jar and
see what reaction you get. If there's a slow, steady
reaction, there's life in the jar.

So what happened?

By filling the jars with sand and refrigerating them,
you created a Mars-like environment. What you
were trying to discover is if there were any living
microorganisms in this environment. The sugar water
heated things up and added a little fuel to the
equation (via the sugar). Living organisms need sugar,
water, and heat to stay alive.

WHY IS MARS RED?

What you'll need:

- sand
- steel wool
- scissors
- water
- a pair of work gloves

How to do it:

Pour the sand into a pan. Put on your gloves, then cut up the steel wool and mix it with the sand. Pour enough water in the pan to cover everything. Check the pan every day to see what color its contents become.

So what happened?

Oxidation is what happened. Which is to say, left to sit in the water for a few days, the steel wool rusted. Steel wool is made from low carbon steel, which is very similar to iron, which also rusts when it's exposed to water. Meteorites from Mars that have landed on Earth have been found to have iron in them. Scientists think that at one time there was water on Mars, which caused the iron in Martian rocks to rust, turning the planet a cool shade of red.

Check out more adventures from the
best fourth-grade scientist ever.

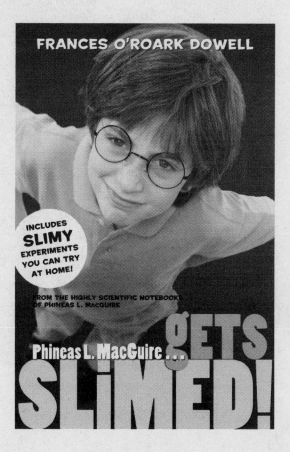

Available now.

chapter one

My name is Phineas Listerman MacGuire.

Most people call me Mac.

My Sunday-school teacher and my pediatrician call me Phineas.

A few people, mostly my great-uncle Phil and his cockatiel, Sparky, call me Phin.

Nobody calls me Listerman.

Nobody.

I mean not one single person.

Everybody got that?

I am currently in the fourth grade at Woodbrook Elementary School. On the first day of school my teacher, Mrs. Tuttle, asked us to write down our number one, two, and three goals for the year. Here is what I wrote:

1. To be the best fourth-grade scientist ever
2. To be the best fourth-grade scientist ever
3. To be the best fourth-grade scientist ever

So far this has not happened.

For example, I did not win the fourth-grade science fair. Me and my best friend, Ben, got an honorable mention.

We made a volcano. It was a pretty good volcano, since I am an expert volcano maker. But these days it takes more than baking soda and vinegar to get a science fair judge excited.

I learned that the hard way.

Today Mrs. Tuttle asked us to take out our goal sheets and review our goals. She says the first week of November is a good time for goal reviewing. She also says most people who don't meet their goals fail because they forget what their goals were in the first place.

"What is one step you can make this week that will help you meet one of your

goals?" Mrs. Tuttle asked. She took a yellow rubber frog from the jar of rubber frogs she keeps on her desk and balanced it on the tip of her finger. "Think of one small thing you can do."

I put my head down on my desk. After getting an honorable mention in the science fair, the only step I could take was to erase my three goals and start over. Maybe my goal could be to remember to take my gym clothes home on Friday afternoons.

Not that I would ever meet that goal either.

Aretha Timmons, who sits behind me in Mrs. Tuttle's class and who won second place in the fourth-grade science fair, popped her pencil against the back of my head.

"Why so glum, chum?" she asked.

"What goals did you put down, anyway?"

I held up my paper so she could read it. "Hmmm," she said. "Well, it's still pretty early in the year. You could do something amazing before Christmas if you put your mind to it."

Ben, who sits one row over and two seats back from me, leaned toward us. "I've got two words for you, Mac: Albert 'Mr. Genius Scientist' Einstein."

"That's five words," I said.

Maybe Ben's goal should be to learn how to count.

"My point is, Albert Einstein, the most

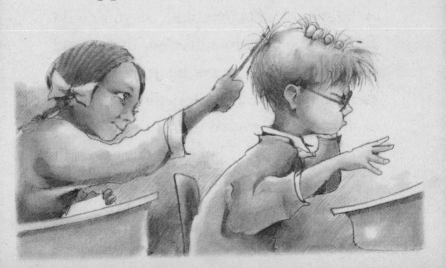

famous genius scientist of the world, flunked math about a thousand times. I don't think he even graduated from high school. He was a complete birdbrain until he was thirty or something."

"I didn't flunk math," I told him. "I just didn't win first prize at the science fair."

"See!" Ben shouted gleefully. "You're even smarter than Albert Einstein."

Ben is not a famous genius scientist, in case you were wondering.

He's a pretty good friend, though.

"What you need is a good project," Aretha said. "For example, if you could figure out a cure to a disease, that would be excellent. I've never heard of a fourth grader curing a disease before."

"Or maybe you could rid the world of mold," Ben said. "I mean, for a fourth grader, you sure know a lot about moldy junk."

It's true. I have always been sort of a genius when it comes to mold. Mold is like science that's happening all over your house, unless your family is really neat and tidy and cleans out the refrigerator on a regular basis.

This does not describe my family at all.

"Not all mold is bad," I told Ben, showing off my geniosity. "In fact, one of the most important medicines ever, penicillin, is made from mold."

"So figure out how to get rid of the bad mold," Ben said. "My mom would give you twenty bucks if you could get rid of the mold in our shower. That's all she ever talks about practically."

Rid the world of bad mold. It sounded

like the sort of thing a superhero would do in a comic book, if comic books were written by scientists with a special interest in single-celled organisms made out of fungus.

I could be Anti-Mold Man, Destroyer of Slime.

Not bad for a fourth grader.

I raised my hand. "Mrs. Tuttle, is it okay to change our goals, at least a little?"

"Revising your goals is a part of the process," Mrs. Tuttle said. "Sometimes we make goals that are unrealistic or not what we really want after all."

"Great!" I took out my pencil and started erasing my number one, two, and three goals. When I was done erasing, I wrote:

1. To get rid of all unnecessary mold in Woodbrook Elementary School
2. To teach Ben how to count
3. To be the best fourth-grade scientist ever

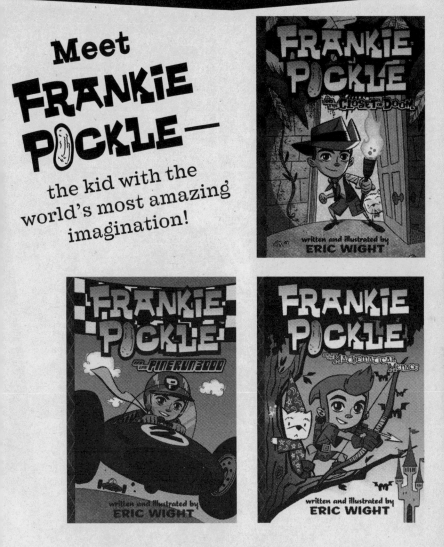